THE CHRISTMAS GIFT

THE CHRISTMAS GIFT

R. WILLIAM BENNETT

BURGESS ADAMS

HIGHLAND, UTAH

© 2010 R. William Bennett

Published by
Burgess Adams Publishing
5406 West 11000 North, Suite 103-311
Highland, UT 84003-8942
(801) 770-2610
www.rwilliambennett.com

Publisher's Cataloging-in-Publication Data
Bennett, R. William.

    The Christmas gift / R. William Bennett. – Highland, UT : Burgess Adams Pub., 2010.

    p. ; cm.

    ISBN13: 978-0-9825606-3-1

    1. Christmas—Fiction. I. Title.

PS3602.E66 C47 2010
813.6—dc22   2010926397

Project coordination by Jenkins Group, Inc.
www.BookPublishing.com
Interior design by Yvonne Fetig Roehler

Printed in the United States of America
14 13 12 11 10 • 5 4 3 2 1

We cannnot live only for ourselves.
A thousand fibers connect us
with our fellow men;
and among those fibers,
as sympathetic threads,
our actions run as causes,
and they come back to us as effects.

– HERMAN MELVILLE

THIS STORY IS DEDICATED TO
all those who have offered an apology,
no matter how difficult,
to those who have given forgiveness,
deserved or not…

...and to those who are striving to do so

CHAPTER ONE

December,
not too many years ago...

"I WANT TO GET HIM and I want to get him good!" the man growled. His face was red and he seemed ready to leap out of his chair.

The lawyer was expressionless. He sat across the table, waiting for his client to finish speaking. It was apparent the man was hoping for some kind of reaction. Instead, the lawyer just listened and said nothing, his empty pad of paper in front of him.

The client was dressed in an older suit that clearly had seen little use. He owned a construction company, and having grown up in the business, usually wore jeans and the logo T-shirt appropriate for days spent on site.

His good nature, familiar to those who knew him, was overshadowed today by an uncharacteristic anger. He had come to the law offices on a mission. He had been wronged, and he intended to deal with it. He wore his dated suit like a coat of armor to show he meant business.

The client pursed his lips, stuck out his jaw, and shook his head. "This guy will never mess with me again."

Another invitation.

More silence.

The client now centered his anger on the attorney. "Well, you're the lawyer; don't you think we can get him?" he demanded.

"Mr. Tanner," the lawyer said with controlled calm, "As I stated, I would first like to find out why it happened…"

"Why he messed with me?" the man

interrupted.

"Yes, Mr. Tanner," the lawyer said as he removed his glasses and ran his fingers through graying hair. "Why he 'messed' with you. Let's discuss again what he did, but then talk about why he did it, and we can decide what would be the right thing to do."

For the next hour, the lawyer listened to Mr. Tanner weave the tale of how he had been wronged. He followed carefully, but still could not discern anything about the intent of the accused.

Mr. Tanner finally fell quiet, waited a long while, and then asked, hopefully, "I think I have a great case, don't you?"

The lawyer stood and walked to the window, put his hand on the sill, and just gazed. His stare was aimless as he looked through the Christmas wreath, identical to the others hanging in each window of the law firm.

"Mr. Tanner," the lawyer finally said wearily, "What happened is not clear cut, and in fact is the kind of thing some people just walk away from and forget. I realize you are offended, and, being a man of action, you want to do something about it. But I think you should first understand why he did this to you. His intent may not be what you think. Perhaps you could settle this by talking it out."

The lawyer turned and peered over his glasses at Mr. Tanner in a way that changed his last statement into a question.

Mr. Tanner was visibly frustrated. "Look, I want to hire you to sue this guy. Do you want the work or don't you?"

The lawyer paused, and taking a breath, said, "Not necessarily. I don't like to see people sue each other over a misunderstanding."

With that, he started to turn back to resume his unfocused gaze out the window, and as he did, his eyes fell on the single picture on the wall.

The pencil sketch was very good in a simple sort of way. The scene was a lake with a craggy

R. William Bennett

shoreline, creating the serene beauty of nature's randomness. In the distance, rolling mountains rose from the horizon in an impressive backdrop. They cradled a single thin but majestic waterfall that cascaded across layers of hills, its final plunge disappearing into the lake.

In the foreground, a weathered dock stretched over the narrow, rocky beach a short distance into the water. At its end sat two boys, feet dangling over the edge, holding fishing poles, seemingly oblivious to the artist as they discussed some item of importance in their world.

The lawyer stopped and looked intently at the picture for a while. He knew this work of art intimately well, having studied each of its thoughtful pencil strokes an untold number of times, and having discovered its subtle images and assessed its many meanings so often that if he'd had any artistic talent of his own, he could have almost flawlessly recreated the piece without looking at it.

Yet today, after contemplating the picture, he found something new – or, at least, something that suddenly enlightened him in his efforts to assist Mr. Tanner. He turned and quickly walked back to the table, sat down, and leaned forward, hands folded in front of him.

"Mr. Tanner, I have an idea. If you'll let me tell you a story – about that picture on the wall behind me – I'll take your case if you still want me to. Do we have a deal?"

Mr. Tanner looked up at the picture, saw no apparent relevance to his situation, and refocused his gaze on the lawyer with a grunt. "I don't really have time for a story. I just want to talk about my case."

"Please," the lawyer said sincerely, "Hear me out. I think you will find it has everything to do with your case." He stared unflinchingly at Mr. Tanner.

Without saying anything, Mr. Tanner leaned back in his chair with a sigh, looked at his watch, and folded his arms across his chest.

He glanced at his watch a second time just to make his point.

The lawyer took this as a sign – a reluctant sign, but a sign nonetheless – to tell the story.

CHAPTER TWO

September
1968

IT WAS FALL, and for Scott, that often meant a new town, a new house, and new friends. About every other year, his father was transferred, so his family packed up, moved out, moved in, and unpacked. This was one of those years.

They adapted well. While it wasn't always easy, Scott and his two sisters were close and his mother helped them focus on the adventure of it all. In fact, Scott would have to confess he liked the new streets, new sights, new bedroom, and new places to explore.

Even making new friends had become a process he was comfortable with. Only one thing gave him a little anxiety – the new school.

In the little society called "school" existed the caste system that thrived in Scott's time just as it had in every generation before him.

There were the jocks who liked to hit each other in the arm in the hall.

There were the nerds who all wore glasses and were friends with either the science or math teachers.

There were the hippies who wore tie-dyed shirts and headbands and who sat in circles on the school lawn at lunchtime, humming or chanting something Scott could not decipher.

The great remaining mass Scott labeled the "normals." They had no clear identity and didn't congregate; they were simply normal.

Scott was a "normal" and content with it.

Despite this, he was nervous the first week of school, as he always was. He worried not so much about fitting in as standing out.

Usually, lots of clues called out the new kid, yet this time his style seemed about the same as the style of the town. Like him, almost all the kids wore bell bottoms carefully gauged to cover their shoes and just touch the floor.

His hair, too, looked about like every other boy's hair – a mass of bangs in the front, long enough to whip to the side with a carefully executed toss of the head.

Likewise, everyone talked about the same – no unusual accent or noticeable slang marked Scott as an outsider. It seemed he might blend in better, with less adjustment, than usual.

As with previous moves, he would find friends in the first few weeks. In the lunch-room, on the playground, or in class, he would run into someone who laughed at the same joke or seemed interested in the same topic, and that person would become his first friend. This friendship would lead to a new circle that shared common interests.

This time friendship would come quickly – the first day – and, as often was the case, it would happen in the lunchroom.

And, as usual, there would be someone, or several someones, who didn't like him.

Scott liked most people himself and wasn't sure why anyone wouldn't care for him, aside from his shortcomings in throwing a long bomb, knowing the cover story of the latest issue of *Popular Science*, or naming all the members of the Grateful Dead.

But with the "normals," these skills and facts were not terribly important and so had never been of interest to Scott.

Still, there must have been something he'd done to stand out, to inadvertently rub someone the wrong way.

This time, the rub also came quickly, also on the first day, and also in the lunchroom. This time, the one who clearly did not like him was Ben.

On Scott's very first day in sixth grade in

this new school in this new town, he was in the lunch line behind a boy who looked three grades older than him.

At first he thought it was a teacher, but he noticed the long wispy hairs that were a poor attempt at growing side-burns and realized this mountain of a kid must be a student.

He would learn quickly that this was Ben – or, as he was known by the students, "Big Ben," "Ben-ja-maniac," "Ben-Hurt," and a myriad of other names.

As they pushed their trays down the chrome runners of the lunch line, Scott could hear Ben making derogatory comments and laughing about the food choices, comparing each to a different item on a long list of unappetizing images.

When they came to the dessert section, Scott leaned as far as he could under the sneeze guard to grab a piece of Boston Cream pie.

Perhaps that movement caught Ben's attention. In any event, he turned and watched

Scott put the plate on his tray.

Ben pondered the pie a second, and then leaned into the dessert section to find another. Scott could see Ben's eyebrows furrow as he discovered what Scott already knew – that Scott had taken the last piece.

Ben never looked at Scott's face. He just reached down, took Scott's pie, put it on his own tray, and walked on, never breaking his conversation with his friends.

Scott was not one to pick a fight, or necessarily run from one either. He had come home with a bruise or two over the years, but frankly, didn't often find many things worth fighting about. That was the case with the pie.

Scott initially stiffened in anger, but then let it go and looked back at the dessert cooler. He picked out a piece of chocolate cake that had been a distant second to his first choice.

He briefly looked at his pie moving down the line with Ben toward the cash register, thought about how much he liked Boston Cream, and then reminded himself it was no big deal. He paid and found a place to sit by himself.

He had only been seated at the end of the long folding lunch table for a few seconds when a boy about his age with freckles and unruly red hair sat next to him.

The boy set down his tray with his macaroni and cheese but pushed it forward, wanting to talk to Scott first. "So, you fed Ben today?"

"Huh?" Scott said, as he looked up with a mouthful of meatloaf.

"You fed Ben. You let him take your pie. Good call."

Scott swallowed, took a drink from his milk carton, and asked, "Why was it a good call?"

"Because you would've let him or you would've worn it. That's Ben Jackson. He's not human. Jake and I checked once and we found out he was made in a lab."

Scott smiled and looked at the boy, who grinned back.

"My name is Andy. Welcome to Maple

Grove Elementary. Beware of Ben, that's all I gotta say."

"Hi, Andy. My name is Scott. And…I'm not afraid of Ben."

"Really? Bobby Cooper said that too."

"What happened to him?"

"No one knows. He just disappeared. We think Ben ate him."

Scott looked at Andy with a disgusted twist of his mouth. Taking a bite of his green beans, he offered, somewhat sarcastically, "Maybe he moved away?"

"Well, his parents did," said Andy, finally dipping into his macaroni and cheese. "But we think they moved because Ben ate him."

"You know, somehow I don't believe you."

Andy laughed, "I don't believe me either, but you're the new kid and we have to see how dumb you are. You didn't buy it, so you pass."

Scott and Andy kept talking as they finished their lunches. After dropping off their trays, they walked out to the field for recess.

Andy introduced Scott to a group of boys and soon they started a basketball game. Scott got the ball and was about to pass it when he heard a commotion and stopped. Looking at the next court, he saw a crowd of kids gathering.

"Leave it alone, Scott," Andy cautioned, but Scott walked over to see what was going on.

He wormed his way through the growing crowd and saw Ben and a cluster of what must have been his friends surrounding a boy they were pushing back and forth. Ben's head stuck up above all the other kids'.

"'We had the court first,'" Ben said in a mocking voice, obviously imitating the taunted boy. Then he barked more firmly, "We play anywhere we want!"

Andy came up behind Scott in the crowd.

"This is what he does," Andy whispered. "He wants what you have, and he takes it. Later, he kills you."

Scott ignored him. The boy in the center of

the group was clearly scared. Without a word, Scott walked into the circle.

"Com'ere," he said to the boy. "Come play on our court." He motioned with his head for the boy to follow him.

The crowd went quiet as Ben stared at the scene unfolding before him. Obviously, Scott had crossed into a place no one in the school had dared go before.

"Whoa, it's 'Pie-Man,'" Ben said.

Scott cringed as he walked away, knowing Ben had recognized him. *This is not good*, he thought. He tried to shrink his head into his body as he walked, but he could not retract it far enough. He felt hot breath on his neck.

"Here to save your little buddy?" Ben asked, loud enough for all to hear.

Scott just kept walking with the boy. When they got to their court, they ignored Ben and started playing. Within seconds, however, Ben was standing in front of Scott.

"We want to play on *this* court..." Ben

said, pausing and pointing at the ground for effect, "...with *your* ball, Pie-Man..." gesturing toward the ball under Scott's arm, "which is now *my* ball."

Ben grabbed the ball and immediately went for a layup, body-slamming Scott to the ground as he drove past him.

Scott lay there as Ben and his friends started to play, then slowly got up and walked off, casting a frustrated backwards glance at his lost territory.

Andy and the others quickly came to his side.

"Hey, way to go! Way to stand up to him!" Andy exulted.

"That was standing up to him?" Scott replied incredulously. "He took our court, he took your ball, he knocked me over, and I didn't do anything about it." He looked back at the court that Ben and his friends had already deserted and said sarcastically, "Way to go."

"Well, most kids just start crying," Andy

said with authority. "Have a breakdown, right here on the playground. They need counseling later. By comparison, you're a hero."

Despite Andy's assurances to the contrary, Scott felt more like a loser than a hero.

CHAPTER THREE

AND SO IT BEGAN. Scott built a new group of friends, with Andy as his best buddy. But every day, there was Ben. Sometimes he helped himself to Scott's food. Sometimes he knocked him over in the hall. Sometimes he pushed his books out of his arms as he walked to the bus.

Scott never knew what was coming, but he imagined that each night Ben plotted the attack for the next day.

He did find that every time something happened, he was surrounded by other kids, who consoled him by telling "Ben Stories."

First, there were the ridiculous claims:

"He's been in the sixth grade for five years."

"One time, my friend saw him beat up five kids from another school all at once."

"I heard the police are afraid of him and had to call in the FBI to arrest him, but he escaped."

"His house is actually built over a cave where he and his gang go down and take kids apart and stick them back together with different arms and legs and stuff."

Then there were the more troubling rumors:

"He was a 'juvie' and spent six months in a detention center for punching a teacher in the face."

"His parents beat him when he's bad. Kids have seen his scars when he's in the locker room."

"He's got a disease in his brain that makes him act crazy and want to kill people."

Scott did his best to ignore these stories.

R. WILLIAM BENNETT

He figured none of them were entirely right, but he was bothered that bits and pieces might be true. Regardless, he did know one thing for certain: he, and every kid in the school, was afraid of Ben.

One day, just before Halloween, Scott was in the cafeteria eating the turkey lunch special. He left his spoon in the mashed potatoes while he picked up his pumpkin-shaped cookie. Before he could take a bite, a hand shot out from over his shoulder and hit the end of the spoon, flipping mashed potatoes up in his face.

He whirled to find Ben and his friends standing there laughing. With the white fluff clinging to his nose and ears, Scott jumped off the bench and stood with fists clenched and body taut, facing Ben, as the entire cafeteria began chanting, "Fight! Fight! Fight!"

Then, Scott did something he had never done before; he said something he had never said before. Soon, he would wish he had kept it that way.

"Ben," he yelled with his teeth gritted, "I hate you; everybody hates you. Why don't you just leave us alone?"

Then something happened. It happened so fast, no one but Scott saw. As he blurted out those cutting words, he stared at Ben.

For a split second, Ben's eyes changed. They were not laughing, nor were they mad. They weren't anything Scott had ever seen on Ben.

They were hurt.

For a moment that somehow seemed to last forever, it was as though Scott had been granted a glimpse into a world full of pain and fear and weariness. The depth of what he saw shocked him.

Yet, just as quickly as the look came, it was gone, replaced with a taunting, sarcastic smile as Ben mocked Scott:

"Oooo, he hates me. I'm so sad. I might not get a Christmas present from Pie-Man."

Ben's gang laughed as they walked away. Scott watched Ben turn, and though he did not hear Ben say anything more, he could swear he saw something different about him.

Whether it was the hunch of his shoulders, the sway of his stride, or something else, Scott did not know. But the way Ben carried himself, he somehow looked insecure.

CHAPTER FOUR

BEN WAS NOT IN SCHOOL for the next few days, which was a relief to Scott. Maybe he had the flu, which was going around, or perhaps, assuming Scott could be so lucky, Ben was suspended.

He had no idea, but he was glad Ben was gone, for it gave him time to ponder what had happened without the constant anxiety of watching for some kind of retaliation.

Scott kept mentally replaying Ben's brief but painful reaction, trying to decipher what he'd seen. It was not a look that would have seemed unusual for anyone else in such circumstances, but for Ben, it was definitely out of place.

The more Scott pondered what had happened and the look he had seen in Ben's eyes, the more he was filled with another emotion – regret.

He argued with himself. Why should he feel bad? Ben had made at least one part of every day miserable for Scott since his very first day at school.

One benefit, however, of the lunchroom confrontation was that Scott's social status had climbed a couple of notches. He had never returned so many "gimme-fives" in his life. He was now known throughout the school, and he was admired (which somewhat offset how silly he had looked with mashed potatoes hanging from his face).

At any other time in his life, he might have enjoyed the uncharacteristic popularity. This time, he was mostly oblivious.

He kept reasoning with himself, excusing his outburst and using all the justifications offered by his friends. It worked briefly every time he thought it through. However, soon after each self-counseling session, the discomfort in his gut returned and stayed with him.

He couldn't seem to get past it, and he was grateful to have something else on his mind as Halloween finally arrived.

Scott, Andy, and their mutual friends had a long debate about whether, at twelve years of age, they were too old to trick-or-treat. They finally decided this was it – their last year.

Accordingly, they spent a small portion of their time planning costumes and put greater effort on strategy: the types of treat bags that would hold the most candy, the streets that would produce the highest yield, and what time they should start in the evening.

They made their decisions: pillow cases were the best all-round solution for capacity and strength; the target would be neighborhoods with medium to small properties where the houses were reasonably close together to speed up the down time between doors; and 6:00 p.m. would be the start time so they would not bump into every little kid in town but would still have plenty of time to get their haul.

The boys bought moppy black wigs, put on their suits, made cardboard guitars, and became the Beatles – with a few extra band members.

The night began with an aggressive attack: the "Fab Seven" started on the far side of town where the homes were old and close together with no fences, allowing for the fast door-to-door transitions they'd hoped for. They intended to be polite at every house but to waste no time with chit-chat.

Many homeowners frustrated that plan by exclaiming, "Oh, the Beatles! Now, which one is Paul?"

The boys would try to explain that no one was anyone in particular, except for Andy. He had brought his brother's drumsticks and was feeling rather stupid for choosing to be Ringo, since no one ever asked about him.

As the evening wore on, Andy threw the drumsticks in the pillowcase and every time someone asked the "Paul" question, he would immediately respond by yelling out "I am!"

He did this partly to get a little attention, but more importantly to get the dumb question answered quickly so they could hit the next house.

As the bags filled, the between-house sprints changed to a walk, and the group occasionally paused under a streetlight to pick out the best of their spoils for a snack.

During one such break, while the rest of the group sat on the curb and began an impromptu candy trading session, Scott casually surveyed the street in front of them. It was the peak of the evening and the many small troupes of superheroes, hobos, and hippies were almost back-to-back as they worked the neighborhoods.

What held his attention was one particular

house directly across from them. The lights were on, the standard cardboard pumpkin and black cat were taped to the window, and the front door was open with only the storm door in its place. Inside the brightly lit front hall he could see a big bowl on a table brimming with candy.

However, as trick-or-treaters approached the house, they stopped and whispered something among themselves. Some sprinted past the property to the next one, screaming in terror. Others yelled something, followed by derisive laughter as they too passed. Still more saw the clusters of children before them skip the home and, shrugging their shoulders, did the same.

Occasionally, Scott saw what looked like an older sibling, accompanying a young princess or bumblebee, stop the child from heading toward the house. Each time, the child looked up at their escort, who, without a word, tugged them along the sidewalk, moving on to the next target.

Once, he heard one of these older brothers say out loud in frustration, "Because! That's why. Ask me about it when we get home!"

"Hey Andy," Scott called. "Com'ere a minute."

"Yes, Guv'ner?" Andy said as he walked over to Scott, using his weak rendition of a cockney British accent.

Scott rolled his eyes. "Andy, that's from *Mary Poppins*, not the Beatles."

"What's up?" Andy asked normally, feeling stupid once again.

"What's with that house?" Scott gestured. "You can see people are home. I can even see the candy from here. How come nobody's going up to their door?"

Andy dropped his voice to a whisper. "Because, that's where Ben lives. Nobody wants a one-way trip up there. Heck, the candy they're giving out is probably stuff he stole from other kids."

Scott kept looking at the house, amazed that

every single group passed it by. "I'm sure Ben isn't even there. It must be his mother handing it out – or not handing it out. Why don't we just go up? They have so much candy she would probably give us three pieces each."

"You can't do that!" Andy scolded Scott. "It's not just the danger – you just can't trick-or-treat Ben's house. He's off limits. Nobody ever goes there. When we were little and our parents drove by, we would hold our breath until we passed his property."

"Why did you hold your breath?"

"I dunno. Seemed like the thing to do."

"Don't you think his mother feels bad?" Scott asked. "All that candy and nobody's knocking?"

"Don't know and don't care," Andy said defiantly. "I just know I'm not going up there!"

"Come on," Scott said. "Just once. We're a big group. Nobody's going to hurt us." He smiled at Andy. "You scared, scaredy-cat?"

Andy replied immediately. "Yup!"

Scott reluctantly gave it up and the boys moved on, following suit with the rest of the groups walking by Ben's house.

Scott looked in as they passed. He wondered what Ben was doing on a night like this. Did he go out with his like-minded friends? Did he hide in the bushes and steal kids' candy? Was he still thinking about what Scott had said to him, like Scott was?

CHAPTER FIVE

SCOTT GORGED HIMSELF with his Halloween treats, as did everyone else. The enjoyment was short-lived. He did not eat a thing all the next day and at one point during the weekend, for a few short hours, committed himself to a life of vegetarianism. By Sunday, his stomach was settling and he looked forward to his family's traditional noon dinner.

However, nothing seemed interesting. Scott picked lightly at his food, lost in his thoughts about Ben. He was curious and bothered.

When he'd told Ben everyone hated him, he hadn't really known that – he'd just said it in anger. However, it seemed as though everyone really did hate him, except maybe the other bullies. Not even candy would draw kids to his home.

"Scott," his dad said after dinner, "come into the kitchen and help me with the dishes."

His father handed him a dishtowel and said, "I'll wash; you dry."

After a few minutes of simple talk about Halloween, his father asked him, "What's on your mind, Scott? You seem far away today."

"Nothing," Scott said.

After a minute of silence, his father asked, "You excited for Thanksgiving and Christmas?"

"Kind of."

His father said no more, which was as good as asking again.

"Okay," Scott said, realizing his father was going to be persistent. "I feel bad about something I said. There's this kid, Ben, who tries to make me miserable every day."

Scott told him about the various encounters he'd had with Ben, finishing, "So, when this thing with the mashed potatoes happened, I told him that I and all the other kids hate him."

His father stopped washing, wiped his hands, and then turned and leaned back against the counter, facing Scott. After a few moments of contemplation, he asked, "So, think about it. Do you?"

"What?"

"Hate him. Do you really hate Ben?"

"Yes…No, not really." Scott shook his head. "But I hate what he does! I hate worrying about what he'll do to me every day."

His father smiled. "That, I get." He then became more serious. "But words can be a pretty powerful weapon."

"I know," Scott said. "I felt like I had a weapon. Dad, when I said it, I saw something that happened so quickly, I don't think anyone else even noticed. It was in his eyes. It was like I hit Ben, even though I didn't."

"Well," his father said, "you obviously hurt Ben, but he's trying to hide it."

"Well, he hurts me every day."

"Physically?"

"No," Scott consented, "not really. He's just bothering and embarrassing me."

"Well, that's not good either. Ben is out of line." His father paused for a moment, and then added, "What do you want to do about it?"

"Oh, I'm fine. I'm not the only kid he bothers, and my friends always try to make me feel better." Scott paused. "Yesterday, someone told me Ben was a runaway from an island of half-men, half-gorillas."

Scott let out a small laugh, expecting his dad to at least offer a smile. However, he was chagrined when he saw the serious, sad look on his father's face. He immediately felt again as he had when he'd told Ben he hated him.

"I'll be all right," Scott said quietly.

"I know you will, Scott," his father said, "and that's important. But that's not what I meant when I asked you that question."

Scott looked up, confused.

His father continued, "What I meant was, what are you going to do about how bad you feel for hurting Ben?"

They sat quietly together. Scott knew where this was going, and his father knew he knew it.

"Scott," his father finally said thoughtfully, "I don't know what makes Ben do what he does, but I do know that when people say ridiculous things about someone, people become...kind of a mob. They don't really think. They jump on some crazy comment and gang up against the person about whom it was said."

Scott told his father about watching Ben's house on Halloween. He winced as he told him how no one would approach the house, just as his father did as he heard it. His father looked at the floor and shook his head.

"That's exactly what I mean, Scott. A few people start a rumor and look what it does. Can you imagine what his family feels like… what Ben feels like? When a person thinks everyone is against them, sometimes they do things to protect themselves and hide their feelings."

"Don't you think Ben deserved it?"

"No, I don't. I think Ben needs to be dealt with, but not that way." He paused, and then said, "Let me ask you something. Why does Ben act like that?"

"I don't know," Scott shrugged. "I have no idea. Nobody does."

"Well, why don't you find out?"

"How?"

"Do you still feel bad about saying you hated him?"

"Yup," Scott said with a sigh. "I feel even worse now that we're talking about it."

His father reached out and tousled Scott's hair. "It won't go away until you make it right.

Do you know how to do that?"

Scott knew what he needed to do and he dreaded it. "I need to say I'm sorry."

"That's right. When you do, why don't you ask Ben why he does what he does? Find a time when he's not around his friends, so he doesn't feel any need to put on his 'tough guy' act in front of them."

"Okay." Then, after a pause, he asked, "Dad, can I take karate first?"

"Scott…"

"I know; I know."

I'm a dead man, Scott thought.

CHAPTER SIX

"YOU'RE GOING TO DO WHAT?" Andy exclaimed in disbelief the next day. "Hey, maybe if he tears your tonsils out first, you won't have to say it!"

The two boys were walking to school when Scott told Andy he was going to apologize to Ben. As he discussed what he planned to say, Andy responded with example after example of what Ben would do in return.

"What are you apologizing for anyway?" Andy asked, taking a new tack. He mocked what Scott might say: "'I'm sorry I didn't have more mashed potatoes so you could hit other kids too.'

"'I'm sorry you had to reach over so far to hit the spoon.'

"'I'm sorry I had the nerve to get mad when you trashed me in front of everybody.'"

Andy got serious. "What's the deal? What was so wrong with what you did? He deserved that, except times a hundred."

"I just don't feel right," Scott said. "Even though he was a jerk, I still shouldn't have said everybody hated him."

"Well, I don't think the score is close to even, and you and every kid in school are on the losing end. I don't get it."

That put an end to their conversation and they walked silently the rest of the way. As soon as they neared the building, Andy ran ahead without a word, leaving Scott to contemplate his problem alone.

However, this day was surprisingly different

than all the days of the last few months. Ben walked by Scott in the hall and did not even look at him. In the lunchroom, Ben was the same old Ben to everyone else, but he didn't come near Scott.

For the next few days, Scott thought that perhaps he would not have to face up to the apology, but his stomach still hurt and he wasn't happy. For some reason he didn't understand, Ben didn't want to see him. And, for a reason he understood clearly, he didn't want to see Ben.

It wasn't that he was scared of him. He felt safer from Ben than ever. It was just that when he looked at Ben, his gut reminded him of the thing he had to do. Finally, he knew he just had to get it over with.

Scott decided he would go to Ben's house so it would be easier for Ben to talk, as his father had suggested. However, since Andy had led them around on Halloween and the neighborhoods were still unfamiliar to Scott, he couldn't remember where Ben's house was. He went to the office after school to get the address.

Mrs. Martinelli, working her post at the front desk, looked up over her reading glasses. "Hey, Scott, how are you getting along?"

"Fine, I guess," Scott said without enthusiasm. "Mrs. M., can I get an address from you?"

"Sure, Scott, whose do you need?" she asked as she grabbed the school directory.

"Ben Jackson's."

Mrs. Martinelli stopped. "Is this about the lunchroom incident?"

'Lunchroom incident?' Scott thought. *This thing has a name already?* He pictured the school staff sitting around with a case file on him, Ben, and "the incident."

"Well, sort of," Scott said, trying to keep Mrs. Martinelli from asking why he wanted it.

"Scott," she said, putting the directory back down, "Why do you want it?"

Well, that didn't take long.

"I need to do something," Scott said quietly, feeling her bearing in on him like a heat-seeking missile.

"Scott, I think you should let your parents handle this. If you'll have your father or mother call, I'll give them the Jackson's phone number," she said quietly.

"My parents can't...shouldn't...handle this. I have to," Scott said with frustration.

Mrs. Martinelli said nothing but virtually demanded with her practiced stare that he supply more information.

Scott looked back without a word. It became a contest.

Scott lost.

"It's like this," he said uncomfortably, "I...I said something to Ben. It wasn't good. I have to apologize to him."

Mrs. Martinelli looked shocked. She sat back, eyebrows arched, lips pursed. Slowly a smile came across her face and her look changed to approval as she reached for the directory again.

"I think it will be okay," she said, still smiling. She took out a slip of paper and wrote down the address. Handing it to him, she added, "He only lives a few blocks from here."

Scott turned to leave, but stopped as Mrs. Martinelli addressed him.

"Scott..." she said, but then didn't say anything else. She just smiled and slightly nodded her head.

The next day was Thursday, three weeks before Thanksgiving. He had contemplated somehow delaying this visit until December, but he knew he couldn't stand it that long. After school, he began his slow trudge toward Ben's house.

While Halloween had been warm, the recent weather had turned suddenly chilly. The leaves were almost all gone from the trees and had dropped so fast, no one had raked them up yet. He scuffed through the piles of reds and yellows and browns blown across the sidewalks, paying no attention to the crackling foliage thrown by his every step. Though he loved autumn, the beautiful, crisp afternoon was lost on him.

He walked slowly, not wanting to beat Ben home, and really not wanting to go there in the first place. His stomach churned inside him. He thought that if he threw up on the way, he would be justified in turning and running home. But, he knew what would happen. His discomfort would just start all over again tomorrow.

As he replayed the mashed potato day and his angry shot at Ben, he cringed, wishing again he could somehow take it back. Whatever happened at Ben's house, he told himself, at least the regret and anxiety that continued to build in him would be gone. He might have a broken arm, but at least he could recuperate in peace.

What should have been a five-minute walk turned into a twenty-minute shuffle.

Scott eventually came to the house and recognized it from Halloween evening. It was older, but well kept, and had recently been painted, the slate blue color standing out against the fall leaves.

Across the entire width of the front ran a covered porch with a double-seated swing suspended at one end. In each window, lace curtains had been pulled back to let the afternoon sun stream in.

The steps up to the porch and the railings around it gleamed with thick coats of carefully applied white paint, while corn stalks leaned against the wall by the front door, a few pumpkins at their base.

The attractiveness of the house fled from Scott's mind as he approached. He felt as though he had ankle weights on each leg while he took the steps to the porch. As he came to the door, he suddenly panicked, realizing he had no plan to let them know he was at the door.

Should he knock? If he did, he would have

R. WILLIAM BENNETT

to open the storm door first. Someone might hear it creak and then open the front door just as he knocked, startling both of them.

If he knocked on the storm door, the aluminum might rattle and make it sound like he was trying to break in.

If he rang the bell, it might not work, but he might not know it didn't work, and then he might stand there for a long time, and they might open the door just to get their paper, or to go somewhere, and they would wonder, "Why is this kid just standing on our porch?"

He had mapped every potential second of the coming conversation, with every contingency he could imagine. How could he have missed this one vital detail?

Finally, in a fit of confusion and fear, he awkwardly used a bit of each approach, knocking on the storm door, ringing the bell simultaneously, and straining to hear if it sounded inside.

After a moment, the inside door swung back,

revealing a friendly-looking woman who then opened the storm door. "Yes?" she asked.

"Hi," Scott said nervously. "I'm, uh…My name is Scott. Is Ben home?"

The woman seemed a bit surprised, but smiled and opened the door wider. "Yes. Yes he is. Please come in."

She held the door for Scott and walked with him to the entrance of a bedroom in the back of the house.

"Ben," she called as she knocked and opened the door. "Someone's here for you."

Scott looked in to see Ben lying on his bed with headphones on. He sat up, saw Scott, and gave a confused but unfriendly look. His mother left.

He ripped the headphones from his head, slapped off the stereo, and blurted out, "What do you want?"

"To talk to you."

"Why? You gonna tell on me?"

"No."

"Well, Pie Man, then what do you want?"

Scott took a breath. This was the longest silence he had ever experienced. Finally, he found the strength to speak.

"I'm sorry."

The room was again silent. After a long time, Scott realized he had been wrong. This was undoubtedly the longest silence he had ever experienced.

"What?" Ben finally said.

Scott felt incredibly uncomfortable and said nothing for a few more moments. He thought to himself, *This is it – get it done!* With that, everything came tumbling out.

"I'm sorry. I'm sorry I said I hated you, and that others hate you. I don't really hate you and I don't think they do either. They're just all scared of you and hate what you do to them."

Scott stopped and breathed in relief. Whatever Ben did to him now was worth having delivered the apology.

Ben looked at Scott without a word.

While his face was completely expressionless, Scott could tell Ben was thinking. He sensed that Ben did not have many conversations like this one.

After another incredibly long pause, Ben lay back on his bed, grunted something that sounded like "Okay," and put his headphones back on.

Scott immediately realized the conversation was over and he was not going to get to ask Ben why he did the things he did. That was fine with him at first, but then he realized he had not done all he had committed to do, which meant the bad feelings would not entirely go away.

Then, he noticed something: Ben had not turned the music back on. He was lying there pretending he was listening to music. *He's still interested, Scott thought. If I can just think of something to say.*

"Well, I gotta go," Scott said slowly but loud enough to give Ben the impression he was trying to yell over his music. He knew Ben could hear him, but he didn't move. *Gotta think of something,* he thought.

Not knowing what to do, he turned and scanned the room for an idea. His eye caught a glimpse of a picture hanging on the wall by the door. It was of a duck landing on a lake with wings outstretched.

It was not a print, and Scott was momentarily shocked to think Ben might have drawn this. He was about to say how good it was when he realized the room was full of pictures not only of nature, but of sports, airplanes and myriad other topics. Some of the drawings were done with colored pencils, some with paint, and others were just black and white sketches.

Though Scott's purpose in finding something to talk about had been to re-engage Ben, he now asked with complete surprise and sincerity, "Did you do these?"

Ben took the headphones off again. "What?"

Scott smiled inside, knowing he had him. "Did you draw all these pictures?" he asked.

"So what?" Ben said defensively.

"Does that mean yes?"

"So what if it does?"

"They're good."

Ben just sat there. He didn't offer a reply.

Scott had celebrated his victory too soon. He had come close, but he wasn't quite at the point of asking Ben the "Why" question.

Resigned and disappointed, he stepped toward the door to leave, but as he did he was shocked to hear a voice call out to him.

"Want to see more?" Ben asked.

CHAPTER SEVEN

SCOTT FOLLOWED BEN to the basement. He looked around as they came down the stairs, noticing there were no racks or other devices where Ben and his friends pulled kids apart and put them back together with different pieces. In fact, it looked pretty much like every other basement Scott had ever seen.

Ben went to a huge dresser and pulled out one of the wide, shallow drawers. He lifted out a sheaf of pictures.

Then he spoke in a way that was about as

"un-Ben-like" as Scott could imagine. With enthusiasm, he fanned through a picture collection of birds, showing him each one, but moving so fast Scott could only briefly look at them. Then he moved on to his bear portfolio, combing through ten drawings in less than a minute.

He put them on top of a table next to the dresser, opened another drawer, and said, "And these are my kid pictures," spreading out a dozen drawings of children portrayed in all kinds of different scenes on the growing pile of sketches.

Scott silently scanned the array of artwork. "How do you do this?" he finally asked.

"I don't know," Ben admitted. "I'm not very good at reading, writing, or math, but I've always been able to draw. When everybody in kindergarten was drawing stick figures, I was drawing people that looked like people. When I look at something I want to draw, I guess I see it like everybody else does. But then I see it again, or deeper or something. It's kind of like I see a story. So I draw the picture, but I try to draw the story too."

Scott saw what he meant. Every picture was excellent in a technical way – shadowing, perspective, texture – all things Scott did not fully understand other than that he knew this art was unlike anything kids their age usually produced. But there was even more to them than that. Each picture conveyed an emotion.

In one drawing, a bear was about to eat a fish it had swiped from a waterfall, but it had paused, looking over its shoulder. In the eyes, Scott could see caution, as though the bear suspected another was coming to steal his catch.

In a different sketch, a mother deer stood eating grass with her fawn. She stood close to her young, their sides touching as they grazed. The fawn's eyes were partially closed, ignorant of anything around it other than the blissful taste of the spring growth. The mother's head was down eating as well, but her eyes were turned up to the fawn, looking at her offspring with both love and protection.

The pictures of people were even better. In one, a child was at the top of a swing's arc. His eyes were closed, his hair blown back, and his smile one of complete joy. Recognizing the features, Scott assumed this was a young Ben.

He looked up at Ben, who gave him a wry smile to acknowledge his unspoken guess.

"When do you get the time to do this?" Scott asked curiously. "Don't you play football or wrestle alligators or something?"

Ben darted an angry look at Scott, then stopped and smirked. "No alligators," he said simply.

"Well," Scott pushed, "what about sports?"

"I don't do sports. I can't."

"Why not? Your mom won't let you? You're big enough to play on the high school team."

"I just can't," he offered with no further explanation and then changed the subject,

R. WILLIAM BENNETT

asking Scott, "Do you like to fish?"

"I don't know. I've never fished before," Scott confessed.

"What! Where did you grow up? It's practically against the law *not* to fish around here."

For the next hour, Ben told Scott stories about fishing. Scott was not so much interested in the stories of fishing as he was in Ben being so interested in telling the stories of fishing.

He was not only enthusiastic, he painted a picture that etched the scene in Scott's mind so clearly, he could almost see the splash of the fish as it was reeled in.

"You boys want some pie?" Ben's mother called down the stairs.

Ben looked at Scott. "You want some? Promise I won't take yours, Pie-Man." Ben grinned and Scott smiled back.

"Sure, I've wanted pie for a long time now."

Mrs. Jackson joined them at the kitchen table. She quietly took in their conversation, obviously enjoying their non-stop talking as they ate their slices of pie.

After cleaning up, Scott walked to the front door to leave. As he did, Ben followed and stood in the hall with a discomfort that seemed to indicate he wanted to say something. However, he just stared at Scott, choosing not to express whatever was on his mind.

It was okay. Scott knew what Ben wanted to say. He wanted to say he was sorry as well, but it was too hard for him.

Scott didn't need him to say it. He could tell Ben was sorry, and that was enough for both of them.

As he left, he realized the pit that had been in his stomach for the last week was gone.

CHAPTER EIGHT

OVER THE NEXT couple of weeks, Scott wandered over to Ben's house after school every few days. Sometimes they played a card game or just listened to records. A couple of times, Ben tried to show Scott how to draw. The whole time, they talked.

As the time he spent with Ben increased, he saw Andy and his other friends less and less. They still met up at lunch and on the playground, but Andy's calls to Scott's house had stopped. When Scott invited Andy to come over, he was always busy.

Likewise, Andy never asked him how the apology had gone.

It seemed that somehow, on the walk to school the day Scott had told Andy he was going to apologize, Andy had drawn a line in the sand when he'd left Scott and run ahead. From that point forward, there was an awkward feeling between Scott and his other friends.

While it bothered him, Scott found satisfaction in getting to know Ben. With each visit, he found himself surprised by at least one positive insight about the boy whom he had feared less than a month ago.

At the end of the second week, Scott came by even though he had not seen Ben in school.

Mrs. Jackson came to the door and looked disappointed. "Oh, Scott, I'm sorry Ben isn't here. His dad had to take him somewhere."

"Okay," Scott said and turned to leave, but Ben's mother called after him. "Scott, could I talk to you a minute?"

He turned and saw gentle pleading in her face. "Sure," he said, and came back up the porch steps. They went into the kitchen and, as usual, she took out a freshly baked pie.

Scott sat in what had become his regular seat at the kitchen table.

Mrs. Jackson cut a slice and, putting it in front of Scott, joined him and took a breath.

"Scott, may I ask you something?"

"Sure," he said through a mouthful of apple pie.

"How did you and Ben come to be friends? I know he's not very nice at school."

Scott hesitated and stopped eating, not wanting to be a tattletale.

"It's all right," she said. "I know Ben probably pushed you around. I've been called into the school many times. That part I can guess. What I want to know is what made you come here."

He told her about the mashed potato day and turned red as he repeated what he'd said.

As he retold the story that had occupied his mind every day for a month, he could see her eyes were full of pain, sort of like Ben had looked, but she kept smiling at Scott.

"So," Scott finished, "I wanted to come say I was sorry and ask him why he did this stuff to me."

"Did you?"

"Yes, I said I was sorry the first day I was here."

"Yes, I know about that," she said. "Ben told me all about it that night when I talked to him as he went to bed. He probably didn't tell you, but that meant a lot to him. I'm not sure anyone has ever said they were sorry to Ben. But Scott, did you ever ask him why he's like this?"

"Nah, I never did. After we became friends, it didn't seem to matter anymore."

That appeared to please Ben's mom. She looked down into her lap a moment, and then asked, "May I tell you why he does those things?"

"Sure." Scott was interested, but he felt a little hesitant. It seemed like this was going to be a big deal.

"Scott, Ben is sick with something that won't get better. It's a problem with his heart. It keeps him from playing sports or doing anything active. If you ever watch him play on the school field, you'll see he only does so for a minute because he gets tired. Then, he'll walk off somewhere to sit down."

Scott remembered that first day when Ben had stolen Andy's basketball. He had taken a few shots and then left the court. Scott had thought it was because Ben didn't really want to play basketball; he'd assumed Ben had just wanted to torment everyone.

"That's how he came to spend so much time fishing in the summer and drawing in the winter," Mrs. Jackson explained. "He loves sports, but not being able to play, when he is so big and knows he could make any team he tried for, makes him mad.

"It worries me because he takes out his anger on others," she continued. "Ben has been through many painful surgeries. Each one has taken months of recuperation and none seems to have done any good. He's endured them bravely, but when he doesn't get any better, he just gets angrier."

"He doesn't really dislike anyone," she finished. "He just acts like he does. It isn't right, but try to understand that he doesn't mean it the way it seems. Everyone is either scared of him or wants to gang up with him as bullies. But when the bullies come over here, they see his drawings and somehow he's not so interesting to them anymore. He really doesn't have any true friends at all."

Scott looked at her wide-eyed, pie forgotten.

"Scott, what I am about to say will hurt you, but it will also help you understand: Ben tells me often that everyone hates him. He knows it inside. I think when you said those words to him, it just confirmed it."

Scott felt like a hot sword had been run through him.

Mrs. Jackson could see it in his face. "Scott, I understand. Those are terrible things he does. I try to explain to him how it affects people, but somehow, between his anger and thinking everyone hates him, he can't seem to stop himself. He won't tell anyone what's wrong. He keeps it a secret because he says it makes him feel 'broken.' So, I let the teachers know what they need to, but out of respect for Ben's wishes, they can't discuss it with any children. The result is, everyone is scared of him and makes up stories about him, and the whole thing becomes a vicious cycle."

Then Ben's mother put her hand on his. "But Scott, you're different. Somehow, you looked into Ben rather than at him. You came here and talked to him in a way that showed you saw that he was a person too, and for these last few weeks, he's been different. He's been really happy for the first time in many years. Each night, he tells me everything you two have done and talked about."

She laughed as she said, "He doesn't want to leave out any details, so he takes almost as much time to tell me as you two spend together."

Scott sat quietly, contemplating all he'd heard. Most likely someone had seen Ben's scars from his surgeries and had made up the lie that his parents beat him. Somewhere along the way, his school absences from his heart condition had been fashioned into a story that he had a sickness that made him crazy. Scott decided to ask Ben's mother about one of the other rumors.

He nervously started, "Mrs. Jackson, when Ben was really mad, did he ever... hit... uh..." Scott could not bring himself to say the word.

"A teacher?" she asked softly.

Scott nodded his head.

Mrs. Jackson hesitated, choosing her words carefully. "He did, Scott, but it's probably not the situation you're imagining. I've tried to educate his teachers about his physical problems and most of them have been wonderfully accommodating. However, there was a gym teacher who did not…"

She paused, obviously having a difficult time saying this part. "…did not try…" She corrected herself again "…did not seem to understand Ben's challenges. While playing basketball in class, Ben kept stopping to rest and each time he did, the gym teacher yelled louder at him, calling him 'lazy' and 'wimpy.' Ben was upset, but was controlling himself by ignoring him until the teacher ran up and yelled, 'Come on, you big slug, do something.'"

She spoke carefully, trying to quote what had happened precisely but without emotion.

"Well," she continued, "Ben had one of his surgeries not too long before that. When they worked on his heart, they had to break his rib cage. It is very painful, and his whole upper body is quite tender for several months afterwards.

We did not want Ben to be in gym class, but he felt he had recovered enough and wanted to be more active. It turned out to be a mistake I blame myself for.

"The teacher, I am sure not realizing what he was doing, slapped him hard on the back as he yelled at him to join the game. The pain was overwhelming to Ben, and to protect himself from another hit, he turned to push the teacher away. The teacher deflected Ben's hand and it slipped into the teacher's face, cutting his cheek."

She took a breath. "The teacher complained that Ben had attacked him. Though many children saw it happen, nobody liked Ben so nobody spoke up in his defense. Ben had to go to juvenile court. Thankfully, a judge made the effort to listen and when it was understood that Ben had undergone heart surgery and was protecting himself, he was cleared of any charges and the teacher was reprimanded for his behavior. For some reason, however, he

R. WILLIAM BENNETT

never offered a word of apology to Ben."

She paused, and then added, "But I have to tell you this, Scott. Ben sat in that courtroom and listened to the awful lies the teacher told about him. He never said a thing, and never lost his temper. I was very proud of him, though I know it hurt him tremendously."

She looked at Scott. "I am sure they make up all kinds of stories about that. If you ever hear one again, maybe you can straighten them out."

She smiled, and Scott looked back, agreeing with a nod of his head.

Mrs. Jackson changed her tone, sounding more serious. "Scott, Ben was not at school today because his heart had a problem. He's with his father at the hospital."

"Will he be all right?" Scott asked.

She said nothing for a minute. Then she smiled and said, "I'll tell him you came by. It will make him very happy."

CHAPTER NINE

THE NEXT DAY, Ben was in school, but he looked pale and tired.

He and Scott did not usually mix much at school, but every few days, Ben would catch him in a private moment in the hall and quietly ask, "Want to come by today? It's a pie day."

At first Scott thought Ben was embarrassed to be seen talking to him, but he had come to realize it was Ben who worried that Scott would be embarrassed to be seen talking to *him*.

This day, though, Scott did not see Ben

anytime after first period, so after school he jogged over to Ben's house and rang the bell.

Ben answered the door. Looking worn out, he smiled and said, "I cut school again today. Come on in."

"You did not," his mother chided him. When she saw Scott, she said, "He was just tired. He needed to come home and rest."

Ben quickly changed the subject. "Want to go fishing?"

"Huh? It's 24 degrees outside."

"I know. Let's fish in my basement."

"You have fish in your basement?"

"Sort of. Come on." Ben walked slowly to the basement, his enthusiasm straining against the lack of energy he obviously felt.

Scott followed, not wanting Ben to see that he had his hand out to help him if he fell.

When they got downstairs, Scott saw that the boxes usually spread across the basement had been stacked against the walls. In the big open space, two chairs were arranged at one end.

Lying on each was a fishing pole.

"My dad cleared away the stuff last night so I could teach you how to cast. We'll have to side cast because the ceiling is too low, but it will work." Ben showed Scott the rubber casting weights on the end of each line.

That day, and the next several, the two boys imagined they were on *the* lake, at Ben's favorite fishing spot in the mountains. Each described the imaginary fish they caught. As they reeled in after each cast, they gave details of the fight they were having against the great trout or striped bass.

Each day, Ben's mother found numerous reasons to come down to the basement, bringing items to be set on a shelf or "checking on something." When she came, she lingered as long as she could to listen to the two boys.

Each day, Ben was intent on teaching him to cast, even insisting they eat their pie in the basement.

One day, as they worked their lines, Ben

kept urgently checking in with Scott. "Do you get it? Do you feel like you can fish now?"

"I think so, but why are you so worried about it?" Scott answered, a little hesitantly.

"Promise me you'll go fishing next summer," Ben said. "When you do, I want you to know how."

"Sure! Are we gonna go to *the* lake?" Scott asked, as he had learned to reverently refer to it.

Ben paused. "Just promise me you'll go."

"Sure, I promise." Scott feigned confusion, not wanting to admit to himself what Ben might actually be saying.

CHAPTER TEN

OVER THE NEXT few weeks, the fishing lessons became less frequent as Ben missed more and more days at school.

One week before Christmas, Scott became enthused with an idea. He went to a fishing shop and asked what was the very best thing he could buy for $10.

The clerk sold him a lure. He described its features, but Scott had no idea if it was really a good one or not. He just loved the brilliant yellow and green stripes and thought that, if nothing else, Ben would think it looked cool.

He wanted to give Ben the gift in school, in front of the other kids. He had long since stopped worrying about what they thought of him. He just wanted them to know he was proud of his friendship with Ben, and that Ben was a kid worth being friends with.

He wrapped the present in appropriate "boy wrapping style" – no effort wasted on bows or ribbons.

The wrapping paper itself was a page from a hunting catalog Scott had found in his family's junk mail. Not surprisingly, he used way too much tape.

The day before Christmas break, he propped the gift on top of his pile of books and carried it around with him from class to class, waiting to see Ben.

He never found him. Ben was not in school, so that afternoon, Scott took the gift and walked the now-familiar path to Ben's house.

As he came down the street, he saw several

cars parked in the driveway and more on the street in front of the house. He walked cautiously up the steps, feeling worried, but told himself they must be having a family gathering of some kind.

When he knocked, a strange man came to the door and simply stared at him.

"Is Ben here?" Scott asked.

The man turned and said, "Karen, it's someone for Ben."

After a moment, Mrs. Jackson came to the door. Her eyes were red and swollen and she did not greet Scott with her usual smile.

As Scott looked at her, he felt his lips begin to quiver. He knew.

"Scott, come in a moment, would you please?" she asked quietly.

He walked tentatively through the door. Several clusters of people were speaking in hushed tones throughout the house, frequently patting each other's backs. The principal of their school was there, standing with his arm around the shoulders of Mr. Jackson, who looked emptily off into nowhere through glassy eyes.

Mrs. Jackson said, "Sit with me a minute here in the living room."

They sat together on the sofa and she took a big breath. "Scott, do you remember what I told you about Ben's heart?"

Scott nodded as tears came to his eyes.

Pausing again, she said, "Well, last night, Ben's heart finally had too much. He passed away in his sleep."

Scott wanted to burst out crying, but tried to hold it back. He managed to speak as he choked, "I brought Ben a Christmas present. I, uh, I…" He held out the gift, helplessly.

Mrs. Jackson took the gift from him, her eyes welling with fresh tears. "Thank you Scott; that was very kind."

His voice faltered. "But I didn't get it to him in time. I wanted to give it to him in school so everyone would see…I wanted him to see…"

He could not finish his sentence as his eyes filled with tears.

Mrs. Jackson looked sympathetically at him. Despite all her pain, she seemed at this moment to feel bad only for Scott.

"Scott, you meant a lot to Ben. Thank you for what you did for him. Your friendship was the greatest gift you could have ever given him."

Scott nodded silently, and then walked to the door, trying to go slowly with measured steps.

Once outside, he sprinted home – harder and faster than he ever remembered running before – somehow trying to outrun his anguish.

He burst through the door and ran upstairs, where he sat on his bed, staring numbly at the floor.

When his dad came home that evening, Scott threw himself into his father's arms and sobbed late into the night.

CHAPTER ELEVEN

THAT SATURDAY, Scott and his parents attended Ben's funeral. It was the twenty-first of December, but Ben's death had put all of Scott's Christmas feelings on hold.

Besides the flowers, the most prominent decorations in the chapel were Ben's pictures. Through the hallways, in the foyer, and around the room reserved for the family, his drawings, paintings, and sketches stood sentinel on their easels like loyal guardians of the young boy, testifying to the depth of Ben's insights on the world, and offering interpretations of his heart.

On a table near the chapel entrance was a guest registry, and by it, a simple frame held the picture Ben had shown Scott of a young boy on a swing, the one that was in fact Ben's self-portrait.

Scott walked in and said hello to Ben's parents. When he shook hands with Mrs. Jackson, he started to cry. She did not release her grip and pulled him close to hug him. After she did, she whispered, "Come with me, Scott. There's something I want to show you."

They walked into the hallway. By the door to the chapel, a long display table had been set up. Arranged on the soft tablecloth were various mementos of Ben's life. His pencils, brushes, and paints were positioned as though Ben had left them there in the middle of a project just moments before.

His fishing license was on top of his tackle box.

Other tokens of his life that Scott had not had a chance to identify with Ben included a wooden train with the dents and marks of years of play, a model car with fingerprints still visible in the excess glue that had been used to assemble it, a telescope, and more.

Scott felt Mrs. Jackson put her hands on his shoulders from behind, gently turning him to face the center of the table. There, a box had been propped under the cloth to provide a display position of prominence above all the others.

Perched on the top was the gift Scott had brought for Ben. The lid was off, leaning against the box, with the hunting magazine wrapping paper crumpled around it. Lying inside, new and pristine, was the lure that was to have been Ben's gift.

In front of the display was a hand lettered sign that read, "Ben's Christmas present from Scott, his best friend of his whole life."

In the funeral, Scott listened to the eulogies

delivered about Ben. There were parts that were familiar to him, thanks to having come to learn a few things about Ben in the past weeks.

Other stories were new. They spoke of Ben's hopes and dreams, challenges and frustrations. They talked about what made him sad and what made him laugh. They talked about his love of animals and fishing and art and sports and the dog he'd loved as a young boy.

Scott realized that if Ben had died a few months earlier and he had come to the funeral, he would not have had the faintest idea who they were talking about. The impressions he'd had of Ben at the beginning of the year, and those still held by most of the students in their school, was of an overgrown angry giant with no heart.

Today, the speakers spoke of a decent young man – imperfect, learning, growing – but with all the dreams of every young man, fighting his way through challenges very few ever had to endure.

R. WILLIAM BENNETT

Scott was thankful he had come to know this side of Ben, but he was sad to think of the parts of Ben he had not personally discovered.

The talks faded into an indiscernible hum as Scott contemplated his and Ben's friendship. Suddenly, something struck him. Up until this moment, he had been surprised at how quickly Ben had changed as they'd spent time together. However, he now realized it wasn't just Ben who had changed.

He had changed, too. He had quit judging Ben. Beginning with Ben's art, he had seen something good in him. After that, he had started looking for good, and he'd kept finding it.

Ben, he realized, was like his art. If you glanced at it quickly, you would see one obvious thing. But if you took the time to study it, more images and more meaning came slowly into view.

After the funeral, Mrs. Jackson again told Scott she was glad he had come into Ben's life.

For the first time, Scott thought, *What if Ben had never come into mine?*

CHAPTER TWELVE

THE NEXT WEDNESDAY was Christmas. Scott's family arose early as usual and began their family traditions. They sat in the den by the fireplace emptying their stockings. They ran with excitement into the living room and gasped at the presents around the tree. They laughed around the kitchen table as they enjoyed the special Christmas breakfast Scott's mother made every year.

Scott enjoyed it all, but in moments of solitude, he felt the sadness and loneliness that had lingered since Ben's passing creep back in.

That afternoon, during their family dinner, he was surprised to hear a knock on the door.

Scott's father answered and spoke to whomever was there for a moment before calling him.

"Scott, Mr. and Mrs. Jackson are here to see you."

Scott walked out, a little embarrassed to be caught still wearing his pajamas. The rest of his family followed him and they all stood awkwardly in the front hall.

Scott's mother broke the silence by inviting them into the living room, where bits of wrapping paper still lay scattered on the floor and parts of a few gifts were spread out in mid-assembly.

The Jacksons sat on the sofa next to the tree. They leaned into each other, huddling against their still-obvious grief.

Scott wondered if it was hard for them to see his home, full of Christmas happiness and excitement.

On his lap, Mr. Jackson held a large, flat, wrapped present and Mrs. Jackson balanced a white cardboard box on hers.

"We are sorry to bother you on Christmas…" Mr. Jackson said haltingly, working hard to keep his composure, "…but we wanted to carry out Ben's last wish." He was barely able to get the words out.

Mrs. Jackson, who seemed to be more in control of her emotions, continued for her husband.

"Ben gave us a note the night after you visited for the last time. He was so weak I think he knew he only had a few days left. He had worked on your present so diligently for weeks and he asked me to open the note if something happened to him before Christmas. When I read it, I found he had asked us to do two things for you."

Ben's father handed Scott the big package as he struggled to speak. He managed to say,

"He wanted us to give you this…" but could say no more.

Scott looked at them both as they motioned for him to open the box. Inside was a framed drawing of a mountain lake. The shore curled in no particular pattern and a thin beach led into brush and trees. In the distance, a regal waterfall cascaded through the mountains and fed the lake.

When Scott looked carefully, he could see various animals grazing, hunting, or lying with their young, all camouflaged in the pencil strokes of the forest surrounding the lake.

But what captured most of Scott's attention was a dock jutting into the lake. On the end of this dock sat two boys, their fishing poles angled out over the still water. One was large, the other slight. The boys' backs were toward the artist as they dangled their feet in the water. Next to each of them on the dock was something too small for anyone else to identify, but Scott knew it was a piece of pie.

R. William Bennett

Though Scott had never seen it, he knew this was Ben's favorite lake, the one he had described in such vivid detail.

In one way, this picture was the fishing trip they'd never gotten to take. But in another way, it was a picture of the trip they had taken every day for the last month in Ben's basement.

Mrs. Jackson continued, "He said it was just as important that I give you this. I have arranged it the way he described. His last night, he wrote a note to you and it's in the box as well." She handed him the other gift with great care, almost as though it contained her last connection to her son.

Scott lifted the lid and looked down. Inside was a slice of Boston Cream pie on a paper plate with a plastic fork and napkin next to it. On the napkin, in Ben's handwriting, were the words:

"I'm sorry. And Merry Christmas. From your good friend, Ben.

CHAPTER THIRTEEN

Back to December,
not too many years ago...

THE LAWYER STOPPED and looked up at Mr. Tanner, whose eyes were as red as his.

After a minute of quiet, Mr. Tanner softly asked, "Well, did you go fishing?"

"We did," Scott said, realizing with a smile that Mr. Tanner had already figured out that he was the Scott of the story. "I went fishing with my dad the summer following Ben's death, just as I promised I would. As we were leaving that morning, my father asked if we could invite Ben's father to come too. I thought it was a great idea, and we went back in the house and called him. He was excited to join us and we went to Ben's lake and sat on that dock and talked of Ben all day," Scott said, gesturing toward the drawing.

"We went back the next summer, and the next, and every summer until Ben's dad passed away twenty-five years later. During that time, I grew up, got married, and had boys of my own who started joining us. Still to this day, more than forty years later, every summer my boys bring their families to the lake and my father, my children, my grandchildren, and I spend a day together fishing. We call it 'Ben's Day.'"

"And Andy?" Mr. Tanner asked. "What ever happened to him? Did you ever become friends again?"

Scott smiled, then leaned over to a phone on a side table and pressed an intercom button. "Hi Crystal. Hey, could you grab Mr. Byrne and send him in for a second?"

Within a few moments, the door to the conference room opened and another lawyer stepped in. In his hair were strands of red that had not quite surrendered to the encroaching gray.

Scott smiled. "Mr. Tanner, this is Andrew Byrne, my partner. We've been great friends for many years, and have been partners in this firm, Stewart and Byrne, since we graduated from law school."

Andy shook Mr. Tanner's hand, noticed his reddened eyes, and turned to look at Scott's as well.

In a gentle voice he said, "It looks like Ben strikes again." He smiled ruefully. "I don't fare too well in the story, do I, Mr. Tanner?"

"I think you're just like all of us," Mr. Tanner said softly.

Andy acknowledged the comment with an appreciative smile. "Thanks, Mr. Tanner. I was like all of us. But I wish I had been more like him," he nodded toward Scott. "You know, that whole experience really taught me something, and it helped me grow up, but that fall, I really missed out."

They were all silent for a moment, and then Andy said, "Well, I'll let you two finish up. Nice to meet you."

As he stepped out, Scott refocused on his client. "Mr. Tanner, I told you this because…"

"Stop, please," Mr. Tanner said kindly. "Your story taught me a great deal too, Scott. I think I will give this man I've told you about a call and talk to him. I'll do my best to try to understand why he did what he did before I take this any further."

Mr. Tanner stood, put on his coat, and began to leave. Then he paused and turned back to face Scott. He could be rough, but he was also a tender-hearted man. He was struggling to say something, so Scott waited patiently.

Finally, he offered, "You gave me a great gift today. When I get mad, or frustrated, I forget sometimes. Thanks for reminding me of how we should always treat each other."

He reached out for a formal handshake, but instead took Scott's hand in both of his. "Merry Christmas."

"Merry Christmas to you, Mr. Tanner."

Mr. Tanner left. Scott stood at the window and watched him as he exited the building and crossed the street. It was clear his prospective client had lost the tension and anger he had brought into Scott's office that afternoon. As Mr. Tanner unlocked his truck and climbed in, Scott could see he was smiling.

Scott turned back to the faded picture and after contemplating it a moment, put his hands carefully on the old frame. He took the treasured artwork off the wall and turned it over. Held to the back with several strips of yellowed tape was a paper napkin, brittle with age. Ben's handwriting was now barely visible.

Scott ran his fingers across the words, mouthing them as he read silently, reconnecting with his friend of long ago.

He then replaced the picture on the wall, straightened it, and whispered, "Thanks, Ben, and Merry Christmas, from your good friend, Scott."

CHAPTER FOURTEEN

MR. TANNER was right.

A great gift was given to him that day. He did talk to the man he had been so angry with, as he had committed to Scott he would do. It actually did not go very well, but Mr. Tanner listened patiently and tried to understand.

As a result, the conversation gave Mr. Tanner yet another gift. He was able to forgive even though the other man was not apologetic. He gave him the benefit of the doubt anyway and assumed something else in that man's life troubled him. In forgiving, he found peace and was able to simply let the issue go.

What Mr. Tanner did not know was that this man would be troubled for some time to come and eventually, years later, would seek Mr. Tanner out to say he was sorry for the thing he had done.

At that point, Mr. Tanner assured him that he had forgiven him long ago, and that he was sorry the man had spent so much time anguishing about it.

As they shook hands, the pain the man carried melted away and Mr. Tanner asked, "If you have a few minutes, may I tell you a story...?"

That afternoon, yet another person heard about Scott and Ben and the turn of events that had so impacted their lives. That man listened with an open heart and was changed as well.

And so it has continued, from one person to the next, and to the next. Because a young boy listened to his conscience, because a caring father counseled him, because an apology was offered, because hearts were softened, and because forgiveness was given, a great blessing was bestowed upon two young boys that eventually fanned out like the splash of a fish jumping in a still lake.

The influence of Scott and Ben's friendship spread like a fabric across miles and generations. Today, wherever in the world you find a relationship that has a thread leading back to those two young boys, you sense something special, something marked by patience, understanding, forgiveness, and love.

Some would call it peace on earth and good will toward men.

Acknowledgments

I WANT TO GIVE MY THANKS to Jane Hughes, who came as a complete blessing to offer her brilliance in editing as well as her artistic talents to create Ben's picture.

To all the wonderful people at Jenkins Group. Steve Bollinger and Leah Nicholson were attentive and caring right from the start. My editor, Becky Chown, cared about this project as much as I did and worked hard to find just the right voice for the many improvements she made. Yvonne Roehler made the cover and the interior flow of the book match its message.

I also want to pay tribute and offer thanks to those who have not only helped me on this project but on my entire life's journey.

To Mom and Dad, who taught values to my siblings and me and, more importantly, lived them in a way that allowed us to learn them by word and by example.

To Bill and Karyn, who tirelessly edited and suggested with insight and kindness.

To Bryan, who constantly fed my enthusiasm in this project, and in all things, to reach for life's dreams and who gave me the gift that got me started on the right foot.

To Christianne, who never relented in seeing me as a writer and whose complete support in my career change helped me enormously.

To Katherine, who has been my number one cheerleader on this book from the very beginning, pushing me and encouraging me.

To Loree, who has stood by me, supported me, inspired me, and believed in me in this and in all things, always.

To my extended family and friends who have provided so much enthusiastic backing of this effort and of me.

And finally, to God, who makes all things possible and taught me to "be believing."

About the Author

R. William (Bill) Bennett grew up on the Jersey shore and in New England. He spent thirty-one years in business, including many years as an executive of various technology and training companies.

In 2009, Bill decided to devote himself fulltime to fulfilling his passion of writing. An accomplished leader, speaker, and teacher, Bill has always used stories of great, everyday human character to cut through the details and reach the hearts of those with whom he works.

Bill has spent thirty wonderful years married to Loree Bascom and they have been blessed with four children, ranging in age from twenty-nine to twelve, as well as two grandchildren.

Bill and his family reside at the base of the Rocky Mountains in Alpine, Utah.

If you wish to contact Bill, he would love to hear from you and can be reached at:

bill@rwilliambennett.com

or

5406 West 11000 North
Suite 103-311
Highland, UT 84003-8942

Please feel free to write!

To learn more visit my website

www.rwilliambennett.com

Notes

Notes

Notes

Notes

Notes

Notes

Notes